For Frau Mair

WOLF ERLBRUCH

MRS. MEYER THE BIRD

ORCHARD BOOKS

NEW YORK

Mrs. Meyer worried about everything. She worried about the buttons on her winter coat. She worried about the cakes she baked. Had she used enough raisins? And Mr. Meyer's hair. Had he combed it today?

Sometimes she worried about the airplanes that flew over her yard. Could one of them crash into her garden and crush her radishes? Would she have enough room in her house for the injured passengers? Occasionally Mrs. Meyer counted her supply of bandages and cotton balls.

Mr. Meyer, on the other hand, was completely carefree. Whenever he would see Mrs. Meyer's worried face, he'd say, "What are you worrying about? The sun is rising, the world will keep turning, it's going to be a beautiful day, and we can't change a thing."

"Yes, yes, I know," she would say.

Yet she couldn't help but worry that a bus full of people would skid around the corner into their front yard. Would she have enough cake to feed them all? And would they like it? Surely those poor upset people would be hungry after traveling so long. At times like this, Mr. Meyer made her a cup of peppermint tea.

Outside, behind the house on a small sunny hill, grew Mrs. Meyer's vegetable garden. She had planted beans, onions, potatoes, and of course peppermint.

One morning as she stood in her garden, she worried about whether the sun would rise the next day and, if not, if she would be able to find the peppermint among the weeds in the dark. It would be so cold! She wondered if she'd have enough gloves and sweaters and whether she should knit Mr. Meyer a pair of wool long johns or, even better, two pairs.

That very morning when she bent
down to see how the peppermint was
doing, she saw at her feet a tiny
naked bird lying on its stomach. Its
blue eyelids were closed, and it was
all alone. Now Mrs. Meyer really had
something to worry about. She forgot
about buttons and cakes, airplanes
and buses, the sun and cold, darkness
and gardens, and carefully picked up
the bird. She stared at it helplessly
until it chirped weakly and opened its
beak and Mrs. Meyer saw a tiny red
tongue moving about. She brought
the bird inside.

She quickly found something that would work as a nest. "I'll raise him," she said to Mr. Meyer.

He laughed. "Whatever you want, dear."

Of course she already had a name for the little creature. She called him Lindberg. Mr. Meyer thought the name was silly, but all he said was "Whatever you want, dear."

What an adventure! Mrs. Meyer had to feed the baby bird flies, worms, and bugs day and night.

The weeks passed, and right before Mrs. Meyer's eyes her little Lindberg grew into a beautiful young blackbird.

One morning at breakfast when Lindy crashed into the side of the table, Mrs. Meyer realized it was time for him to fly. She opened the window, but he didn't budge. She took him outside and tried her hardest to look like a mother blackbird, but he ignored her. She began to worry. What could be wrong? Was he strong enough? Had she fed him enough worms? Suddenly she had an idea.

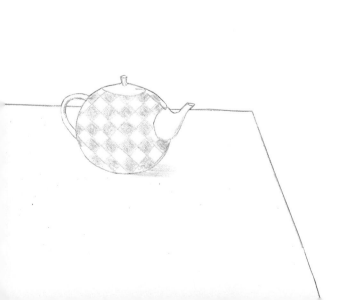

She stuck Lindy in her apron pocket and ran up to the garden. Carefully, branch by branch, she climbed the cherry tree, then settled on a sturdy limb, quite out of breath. She wasn't used to doing this sort of thing.

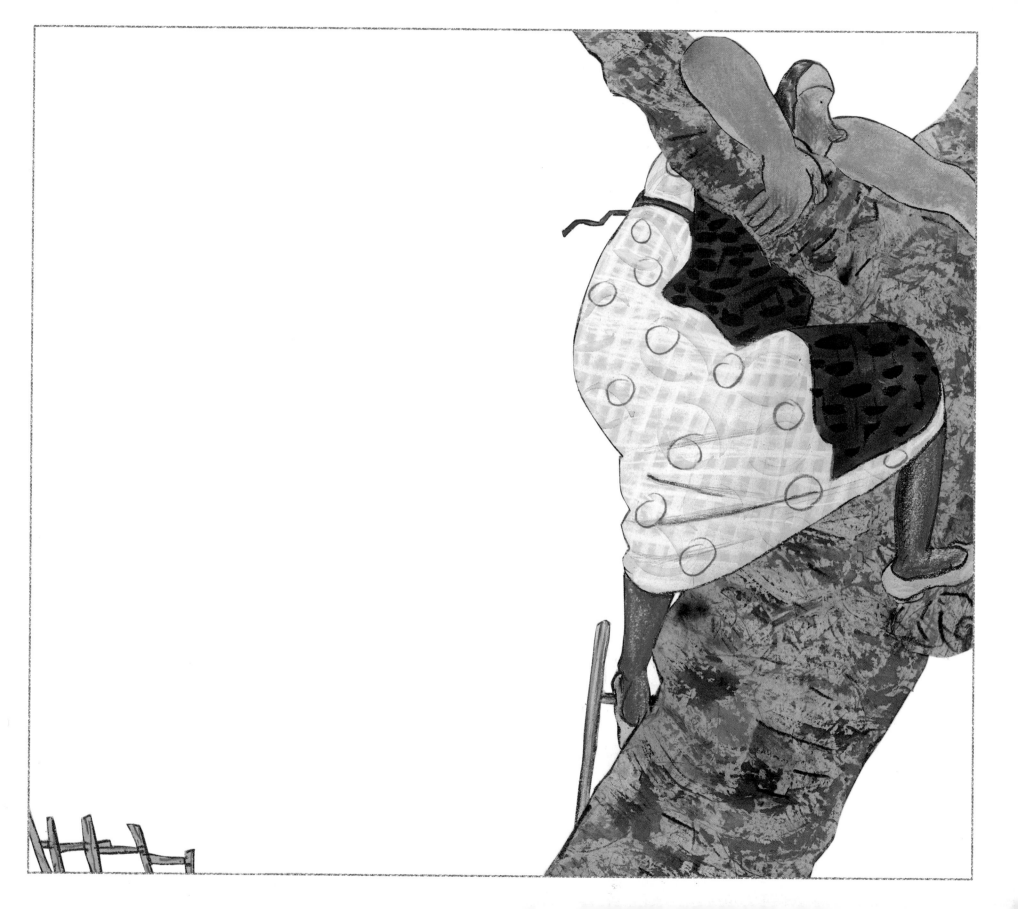

Taking the young bird from her apron pocket, she placed him next to her. Then she began flapping her arms, hoping that the little bird would do the same. But he did not. He only looked at her. Mrs. Meyer threw up her hands and made her worried face.

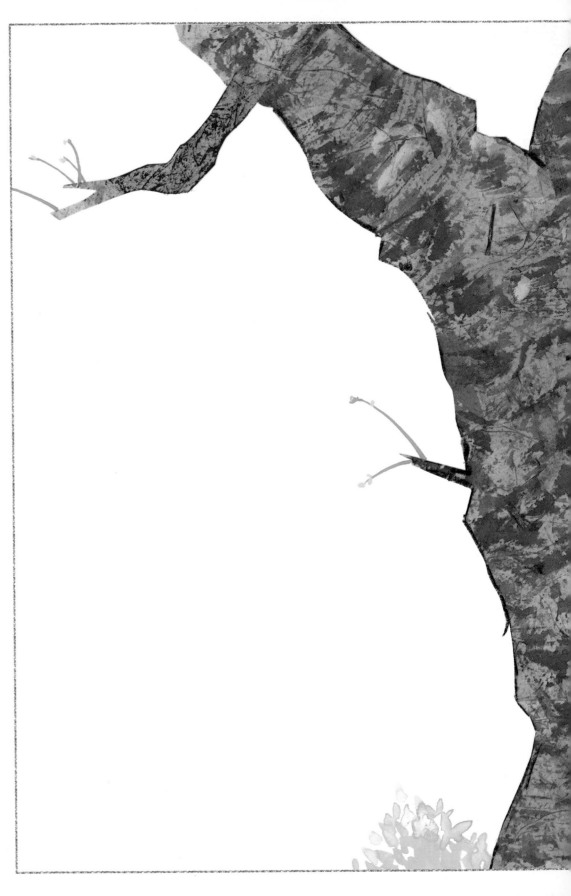

Had she fed Lindy the wrong bugs?
Or was he really a small penguin?
And if he really was, how did he
end up in her garden? She looked
out from her branch, down over
the meadow, across to the forest,
and up to the sky. Lindy looked
with her. The morning sun shone
over the rolling fields below.
A few late-blooming daffodils
glistened. Everything was still.
Mrs. Meyer was suddenly
overcome with feeling. And then
she knew what she had to do.

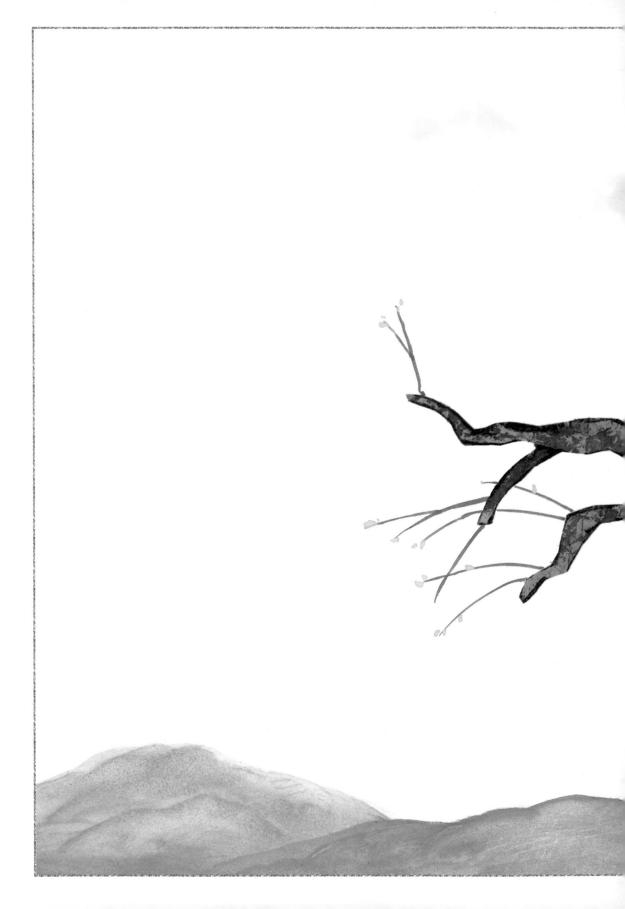

She took a deep breath, spread her arms, stepped off the branch and into the air. A gentle breeze caught and held her, not high in the sky but somewhere in the middle between the treetop and the earth below. The blackbird ruffled his feathers. Mrs. Meyer clumsily landed back on the branch and looked at Lindy expectantly. He fluttered his wings but didn't leave the tree.

Mrs. Meyer couldn't wait any longer. She nudged him off the branch and into the air, where, sure enough, he began to fly. Mrs. Meyer followed.

Together Mrs. Meyer and Lindberg flew down over the meadow, across to the forest, and up to the sky.

Later they returned home for
a cup of tea.

Orchard Books, 95 Madison Avenue, New York, NY 10016

Manufactured in the United States of America
Printed by Barton Press, Inc.   Bound by Horowitz/Rae

10 9 8 7 6 5 4 3 2 1

The text of this book is set in 20 pt. Cloister.

Library of Congress Cataloging-in-Publication Data
Erlbruch, Wolf.
[Frau Meier, die Amsel. English]
Mrs. Meyer, the bird / Wolf Erlbruch ; [adapted from the German
by Sabina Magyar and Susan Rich].—1st American ed.
p.   cm.
Summary: Mrs. Meyer, who worries excessively about everything,
tries to help a young bird learn how to fly and discovers
the thrill of flying herself.
ISBN 0-531-30017-X. —   ISBN 0-531-33017-6 (lib. bdg.)
[1. Birds—Fiction. 2. Flight—Fiction. 3. Worry—Fiction.]
I. Magyar, Sabina. II. Rich, Susan. III. Title.
PZ7.E72594Mr 1997 [E]—dc20   96-41758